POEMS TO SEE BY

A Comic Artist
Interprets Great Poetry

Julian Peters

PLOUGH PUBLISHING HOUSE

Published by Plough Publishing House
Walden, New York
Robertsbridge, England
Elsmore, Australia
www.plough.com

ISBN: 978-0-874-86318-5

24 23 22 21 20   1 2 3 4 5 6 7 8

A catalog record for this book is available from the British Library.

Library of Congress Cataloging-in-Publication Data
Names: Peters, Julian, illustrator.
Title: Poems to see by : a comic artist interprets great poetry / Julian Peters.
Description: Walden, New York : Plough Publishing House, 2020. | Audience: Grades 10-12
    | Summary: "A fresh twist on 24 classics, these visual interpretations by comic artist Julian
    Peters will change the way you see the world"-- Provided by publisher.
Identifiers: LCCN 2019058661 (print) | LCCN 2019058662 (ebook) | ISBN 9780874863185
    (hardback) | ISBN 9780874863192 (ebook)
Subjects: LCSH: Poetry--Collections.
Classification: LCC PN6101 .P498 2020 (print) | LCC PN6101 (ebook) | DDC 808.81--dc23
LC record available at https://lccn.loc.gov/2019058661
LC ebook record available at https://lccn.loc.gov/2019058662

Printed in the United States of America

Contents

To Ignazio "Cetto" Cattaneo (1939–2006),
who at a crucial time in my life passed on
to me his passion for comics.

About the artist: Julian Peters is an illustrator and comic book artist living in Montreal, Canada, who specializes in adapting classical poems into graphic art. His work has been exhibited internationally and published in several poetry and graphic art collections. Peters holds a master's degree in art history and, in 2015, served as Cartoonist in Residence at Victoria University in Wellington, New Zealand.

Preface

Poetry and comics may seem like an unlikely combination, but the two art forms actually share a number of common elements. For starters, both the poet and the comic artist are concerned with the notion of rhythm – the beats created by the stressed and unstressed syllables and line breaks, or by the arrangement of comics panels and dialogue balloons. There is also the regular repetition of visual elements throughout a comic, which can be compared to the use of rhyme in poetry – take for example a Peanuts cartoon beginning and ending with the same image of Snoopy lying atop his doghouse. Perhaps the most significant parallel, though, at least in relation to this book, is the way both poetry and comics make use of the expressive potential of juxtaposition. In poetry, it is very often in the bringing together of two or more disparate images or concepts that the poetic spark is struck (as in, for example, T. S. Eliot's description of the evening "spread out against the sky / like a patient etherized upon a table"). In a comic, meaning is often communicated in the contrast between successive panels, as well as in the contrast between the words and the images.

The poetry comics included in this book set out to adapt or, it could be said, translate twenty-four great English-language poems of the last two centuries into the visual language of comics. In the years since I began creating such works, I have often been contacted by teachers who tell me they are using them in their poetry classes. I'm delighted to think that one of my comics may have helped students to better understand a poem, or perhaps clarify their own interpretation of a poem, even if it differs significantly from my own, which is obviously only one of thousands. (As much as it's true that a picture is worth a thousand words, it's also the case that a single word can conjure up as many pictures as there are people who read it.)

I must confess, however, that my own motivation in creating these works had little to do with their potential educational uses. The truth is, I did it all for love of beauty. A beautiful poem is pretty much the most beautiful creation I can imagine. And the thing with beauty is that we as human beings are rarely content to simply enjoy it for what it is. If a beautiful stranger catches our eye, we wish we had the courage to go up and say hello. If we come upon a beautiful view, our immediate instinct is to take a picture of it (preferably with ourselves in it). If we hear a beautiful piece of music, we wish we could somehow live inside of it. And though in the end we can never quite hold on to beauty in the way it seems to call upon us to do, that will never stop human beings from trying. In setting out to turn beautiful poetry into comics, I wanted to pay tribute to the way these poems made me feel, to spend time with them, to pull them in as close to me as possible in the way that, as someone who draws comics, felt the most natural.

Julian Peters
Montreal
November 2019

Seeing Yourself

"HOPE" IS THE THING
WITH FEATHERS—

THAT PERCHES IN
THE SOUL—

AND SINGS THE TUNE
WITHOUT THE WORDS—

AND NEVER STOPS—
AT ALL—

AND SWEETEST – IN THE
GALE – IS HEARD –

AND SORE MUST BE
THE STORM –

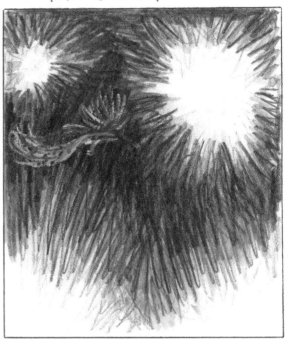

THAT COULD ABASH THE LITTLE BIRD
THAT KEPT SO MANY WARM –

I'VE HEARD IT IN THE
CHILLEST LAND—

AND ON THE STRANGEST
SEA—

YET —NEVER— IN EXTREMITY,
IT ASKED A CRUMB —OF ME.

"Hope" Is the Thing with Feathers

Emily Dickinson

"Hope" is the thing with feathers –
That perches in the soul –
And sings the tune without the words –
And never stops – at all –

And sweetest – in the Gale – is heard –
And sore must be the storm –
That could abash the little Bird
That kept so many warm –

I've heard it in the chillest land –
And on the strangest Sea –
Yet – never – in Extremity,
It asked a crumb – of me.

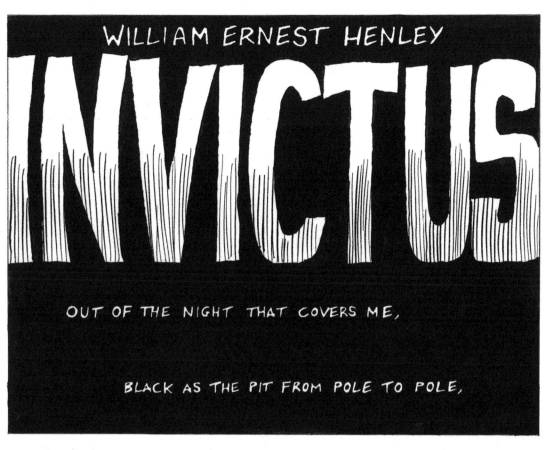

WILLIAM ERNEST HENLEY
INVICTUS

OUT OF THE NIGHT THAT COVERS ME,

BLACK AS THE PIT FROM POLE TO POLE,

I THANK WHATEVER GODS MAY BE

FOR MY UNCONQUERABLE SOUL.

IN THE FELL CLUTCH OF
CIRCUMSTANCE

I HAVE NOT WINCED NOR
CRIED ALOUD.

UNDER THE BLUDGEONINGS OF CHANCE

MY HEAD IS BLOODY,
BUT UNBOWED.

BEYOND THIS PLACE OF WRATH AND TEARS

LOOMS BUT THE HORROR OF THE SHADE,

AND YET THE MENACE
OF THE YEARS

FINDS, AND SHALL FIND,
ME UNAFRAID.

IT MATTERS NOT HOW
STRAIT THE GATE,

HOW CHARGED WITH
PUNISHMENTS THE SCROLL,

I AM THE MASTER
OF MY FATE:

I AM THE CAPTAIN OF MY SOUL.

Invictus

William Ernest Henley

Out of the night that covers me,
    Black as the Pit from pole to pole,
I thank whatever gods may be
    For my unconquerable soul.

In the fell clutch of circumstance
    I have not winced nor cried aloud.
Under the bludgeonings of chance
    My head is bloody, but unbowed.

Beyond this place of wrath and tears
    Looms but the Horror of the shade,
And yet the menace of the years
    Finds, and shall find, me unafraid.

It matters not how strait the gate,
    How charged with punishments the scroll,
I am the master of my fate:
    I am the captain of my soul.

CAGED BIRD

by MAYA ANGELOU

A FREE BIRD LEAPS

ON THE BACK OF THE WIND

AND FLOATS DOWNSTREAM

TILL THE CURRENT ENDS

AND DIPS HIS WING

IN THE ORANGE SUN RAYS

AND DARES TO CLAIM THE SKY.

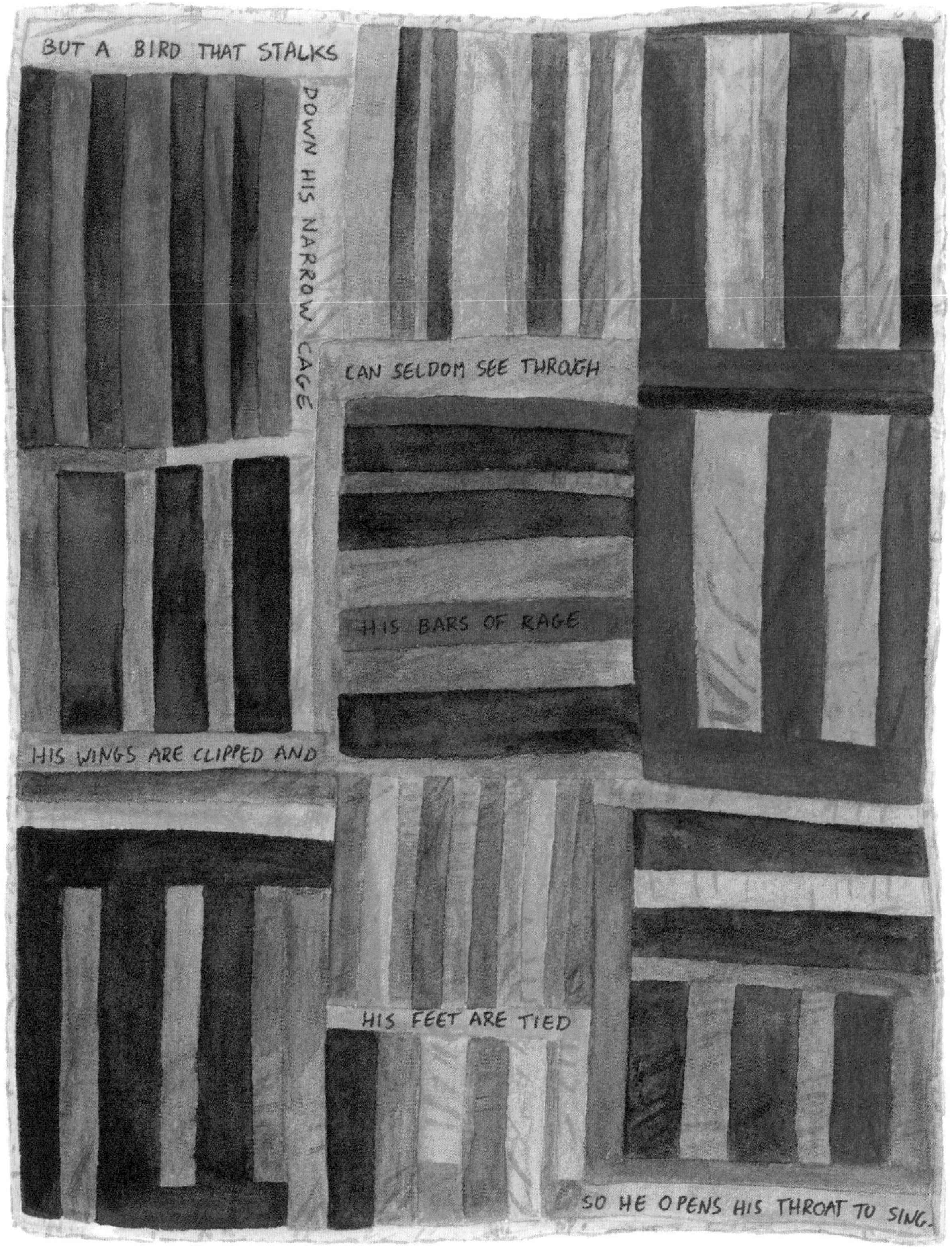
BUT A BIRD THAT STALKS
DOWN HIS NARROW CAGE
CAN SELDOM SEE THROUGH
HIS BARS OF RAGE
HIS WINGS ARE CLIPPED AND
HIS FEET ARE TIED
SO HE OPENS HIS THROAT TO SING.

THE FREE BIRD THINKS OF ANOTHER BREEZE

AND THE TRADE WINDS SOFT THROUGH THE SIGHING TREES

AND THE FAT WORMS WAITING ON A DAWN BRIGHT LAWN

AND HE NAMES THE SKY HIS OWN

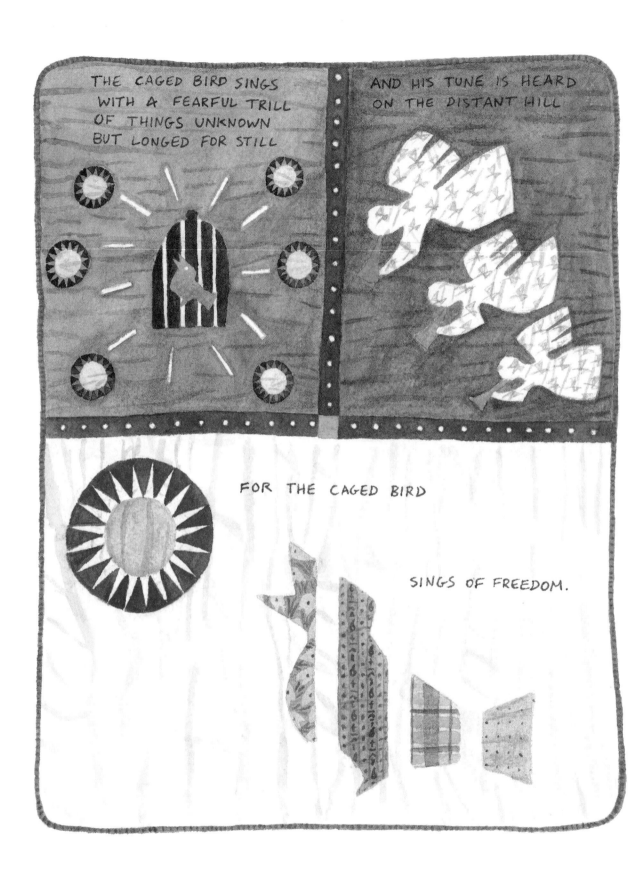

CAGED BIRD

Maya Angelou

A free bird leaps
on the back of the wind
and floats downstream
till the current ends
and dips his wing
in the orange sun rays
and dares to claim the sky.

But a bird that stalks
down his narrow cage
can seldom see through
his bars of rage
his wings are clipped and
his feet are tied
so he opens his throat to sing.

The caged bird sings
with a fearful trill
of things unknown
but longed for still
and his tune is heard
on the distant hill
for the caged bird
sings of freedom.

The free bird thinks of another breeze
and the trade winds soft through the sighing trees
and the fat worms waiting on a dawn bright lawn
and he names the sky his own

But a caged bird stands on the grave of dreams
his shadow shouts on a nightmare scream
his wings are clipped and his feet are tied
so he opens his throat to sing.

The caged bird sings
with a fearful trill
of things unknown
but longed for still
and his tune is heard
on the distant hill
for the caged bird
sings of freedom.

e. e. cummings

may my heart always
be open to little

birds who are the
secrets of living

whatever they sing is better than to know

and if men should not hear them men are old

may my mind stroll about
hungry

and fearless and thirsty
and supple

and even if it's sunday may i be wrong

for whenever men are right they are not young

and may myself do
nothing usefully

and love yourself so
more than truly

there's never been quite such a fool who could fail

pulling all the sky over him with one smile

MAY MY HEART ALWAYS BE OPEN

e.e. cummings

may my heart always be open to little
birds who are the secrets of living
whatever they sing is better than to know
and if men should not hear them men are old

may my mind stroll about hungry
and fearless and thirsty and supple
and even if it's sunday may i be wrong
for whenever men are right they are not young

and may myself do nothing usefully
and love yourself so more than truly
there's never been quite such a fool who could fail
pulling all the sky over him with one smile

Seeing Others

SOMEWHERE OR OTHER — by CHRISTINA ROSSETTI

SOMEWHERE OR OTHER THERE MUST SURELY BE

THE FACE NOT SEEN, THE VOICE NOT HEARD,

THE HEART THAT NOT,YET—
NEVER YET – AH ME! YET—

MADE ANSWER TO MY WORD.

SOMEWHERE OR OTHER, MAY BE NEAR OR FAR;

PAST LAND AND SEA,
CLEAN OUT OF SIGHT;

BEYOND THE WANDERING MOON,
BEYOND THE STAR

THAT TRACKS HER NIGHT BY NIGHT.

SOMEWHERE OR OTHER, MAY BE FAR OR NEAR;

WITH JUST A WALL, A HEDGE, BETWEEN;

WITH JUST THE LAST LEAVES OF THE DYING YEAR

FALLEN
ON A
TURF
GROWN
GREEN.

SOMEWHERE OR OTHER

Christina Rossetti

Somewhere or other there must surely be
The face not seen, the voice not heard,
The heart that not yet—never yet—ah me!
Made answer to my word.

Somewhere or other, may be near or far;
Past land and sea, clean out of sight;
Beyond the wandering moon, beyond the star
That tracks her night by night.

Somewhere or other, may be far or near;
With just a wall, a hedge, between;
With just the last leaves of the dying year
Fallen on a turf grown green.

THOSE WINTER SUNDAYS   by ROBERT HAYDEN

SUNDAYS TOO MY FATHER GOT UP EARLY

AND PUT HIS CLOTHES ON
IN THE BLUEBLACK COLD,

THEN WITH CRACKED HANDS THAT ACHED
FROM LABOR IN THE WEEKDAY WEATHER MADE

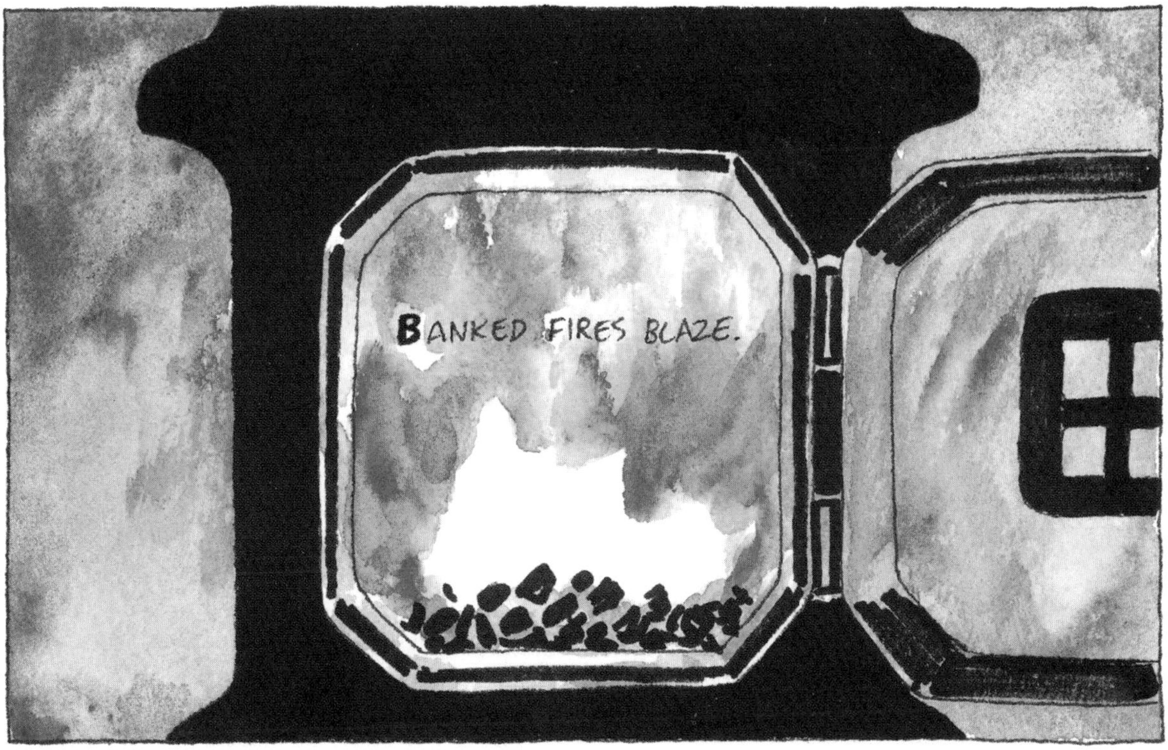
BANKED FIRES BLAZE.

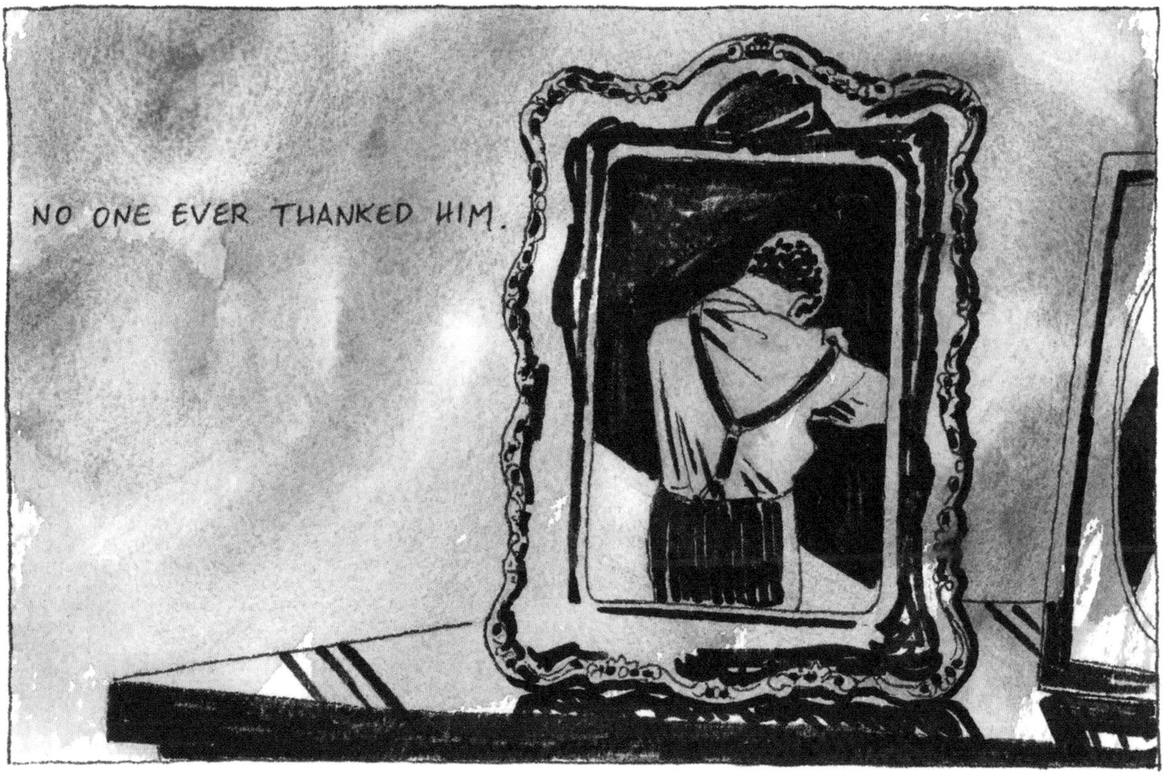
NO ONE EVER THANKED HIM.

I'D WAKE AND HEAR THE COLD SPLINTERING, BREAKING.

WHEN THE ROOMS WERE WARM, HE'D CALL,

AND SLOWLY I WOULD RISE AND DRESS,

FEARING THE CHRONIC ANGERS OF THAT HOUSE,

SPEAKING INDIFFERENTLY TO HIM,

WHO HAD DRIVEN OUT THE COLD

THOSE WINTER SUNDAYS

Robert Hayden

Sundays too my father got up early
and put his clothes on in the blueblack cold,
then with cracked hands that ached
from labor in the weekday weather made
banked fires blaze. No one ever thanked him.

I'd wake and hear the cold splintering, breaking.
When the rooms were warm, he'd call,
and slowly I would rise and dress,
fearing the chronic angers of that house,

Speaking indifferently to him,
who had driven out the cold
and polished my good shoes as well.
What did I know, what did I know
of love's austere and lonely offices?

PETALS ON A WET, BLACK BOUGH.

THE APPARITION OF THESE FACES IN THE CROWD

IN A STATION OF THE METRO

In a Station of the Metro

Ezra Pound

The apparition of these faces in the crowd:
Petals on a wet, black bough.

WHEN YOU ARE OLD

BY WILLIAM BUTLER YEATS

WHEN YOU ARE OLD AND GREY AND FULL OF SLEEP,

AND NODDING BY THE FIRE, TAKE DOWN THIS BOOK,

AND SLOWLY READ,

AND DREAM OF THE SOFT LOOK

YOUR EYES HAD ONCE,

AND OF THEIR SHADOWS DEEP;

HOW MANY LOVED YOUR MOMENTS OF GLAD GRACE,

AND LOVED YOUR BEAUTY WITH LOVE FALSE OR TRUE,

BUT ONE MAN LOVED THE PILGRIM SOUL IN YOU,

AND LOVED THE SORROWS OF YOUR CHANGING FACE;

AND BENDING DOWN BESIDE THE GLOWING BARS,

MURMUR, A LITTLE SADLY, HOW LOVE FLED

WHEN YOU ARE OLD

William Butler Yeats

When you are old and grey and full of sleep,
And nodding by the fire, take down this book,
And slowly read, and dream of the soft look
Your eyes had once, and of their shadows deep;

How many loved your moments of glad grace,
And loved your beauty with love false or true,
But one man loved the pilgrim soul in you,
And loved the sorrows of your changing face;

And bending down beside the glowing bars,
Murmur, a little sadly, how Love fled
And paced upon the mountains overhead
And hid his face amid a crowd of stars.

Seeing Art

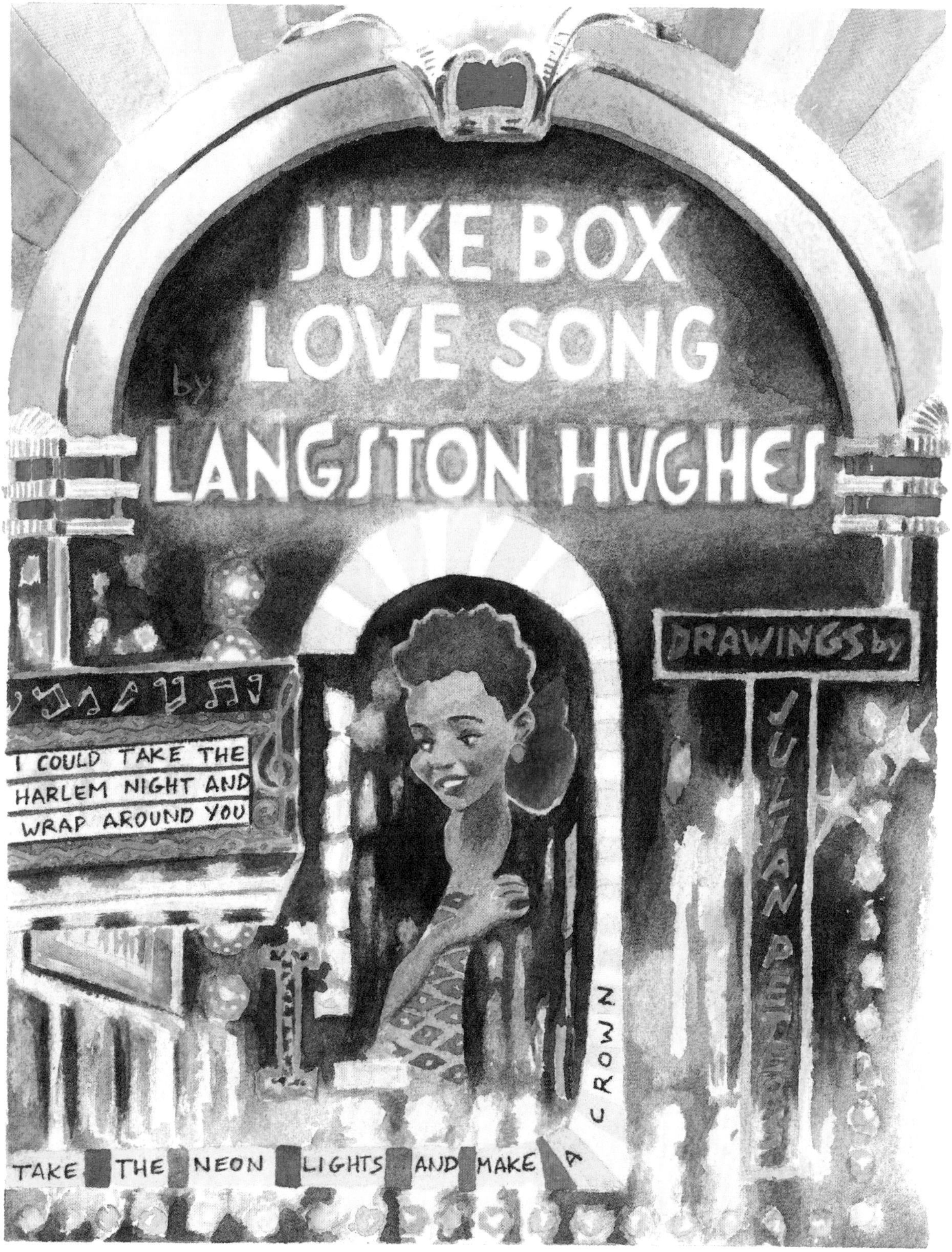
JUKE BOX
LOVE SONG
by
LANGSTON HUGHES
DRAWINGS by
JULIAN PETERS
I COULD TAKE THE
HARLEM NIGHT AND
WRAP AROUND YOU
TAKE THE NEON LIGHTS AND MAKE A CROWN

TAKE THE LENOX AVENUE BUSSES,

TAXIS,

SUBWAYS,

AND FOR YOUR LOVE SONG TONE THEIR RUMBLE DOWN.

TAKE HARLEM'S HEARTBEAT,

MAKE A DRUMBEAT,

PUT IT ON A RECORD, LET IT WHIRL,

AND WHILE WE LISTEN TO IT PLAY,

DANCE WITH YOU, MY SWEET BROWN HARLEM GIRL.

JUKE BOX LOVE SONG

Langston Hughes

I could take the Harlem night
and wrap around you,
Take the neon lights and make a crown,
Take the Lenox Avenue busses,
Taxis, subways,
And for your love song tone their rumble down.
Take Harlem's heartbeat,
Make a drumbeat,
Put it on a record, let it whirl,
And while we listen to it play,
Dance with you till day—
Dance with you, my sweet brown Harlem girl.

MUSÉE DES BEAUX ARTS

by W. H. AUDEN

ABOUT SUFFERING THEY WERE NEVER WRONG,

THE OLD MASTERS: HOW WELL THEY UNDERSTOOD

ITS HUMAN POSITION: HOW IT TAKES PLACE
WHILE SOMEONE ELSE IS EATING OR OPENING A WINDOW OR JUST
    WALKING DULLY ALONG;

HOW, WHEN THE AGED ARE REVERENTLY, PASSIONATELY WAITING
FOR THE MIRACULOUS BIRTH, THERE ALWAYS MUST BE
CHILDREN WHO DID NOT SPECIALLY WANT IT TO HAPPEN, SKATING
ON A POND AT THE EDGE OF THE WOOD:

THEY NEVER FORGOT
THAT EVEN THE DREADFUL MARTYRDOM MUST RUN ITS COURSE
ANYHOW IN A CORNER, SOME UNTIDY SPOT
WHERE THE DOGS GO ON WITH THEIR DOGGY LIFE AND THE TORTURER'S HORSE
SCRATCHES ITS INNOCENT BEHIND ON A TREE.

IN BRUEGHEL'S ICARUS, FOR INSTANCE: HOW EVERYTHING TURNS AWAY

QUITE LEISURELY FROM THE
DISASTER; THE PLOUGHMAN MAY

HAVE HEARD THE SPLASH, THE
FORSAKEN CRY,

BUT FOR HIM IT WAS NOT AN
IMPORTANT FAILURE; THE SUN SHONE

AS IT HAD TO ON THE WHITE LEGS
DISAPPEARING INTO THE GREEN

WATER, AND THE EXPENSIVE DELICATE
SHIP THAT MUST HAVE SEEN

SOMETHING AMAZING, A BOY
FALLING OUT OF THE SKY,

HAD SOMEWHERE TO GET TO AND SAILED CALMLY ON.

MUSÉE DES BEAUX ARTS

W. H. Auden

About suffering they were never wrong,
The Old Masters: how well they understood
Its human position; how it takes place
While someone else is eating or opening a window or just
walking dully along;
How, when the aged are reverently, passionately waiting
For the miraculous birth, there always must be
Children who did not specially want it to happen, skating
On a pond at the edge of the wood:
They never forgot
That even the dreadful martyrdom must run its course
Anyhow in a corner, some untidy spot
Where the dogs go on with their doggy
life and the torturer's horse
Scratches its innocent behind on a tree.

In Breughel's Icarus, for instance: how everything turns away
Quite leisurely from the disaster; the ploughman may
Have heard the splash, the forsaken cry,
But for him it was not an important failure; the sun shone
As it had to on the white legs disappearing into the green
Water; and the expensive delicate ship that must have seen
Something amazing, a boy falling out of the sky,
had somewhere to get to and sailed calmly on.

THE GIVEN NOTE

BY SEAMUS HEANEY

ON THE MOST WESTERLY BLASKET

IN A DRY-STONE HUT

HE GOT THIS AIR OUT OF THE NIGHT.

STRANGE NOISES WERE HEARD
BY OTHERS WHO FOLLOWED, BITS OF A TUNE
COMING IN ON LOUD WEATHER

THOUGH NOTHING LIKE MELODY.
HE BLAMED THEIR FINGERS AND EAR
AS UNPRACTICED, THEIR FIDDLING EASY

FOR HE HAD GONE ALONE
INTO THE ISLAND

AND BROUGHT BACK THE WHOLE THING.

THE HOUSE THROBBED LIKE HIS FULL VIOLIN.

SO WHETHER HE CALLS IT SPIRIT MUSIC

OR NOT, I DON'T CARE. HE TOOK IT

OUT OF WIND OFF MID-ATLANTIC.

THE GIVEN NOTE

Seamus Heaney

On the most westerly Blasket
In a dry-stone hut
He got this air out of the night.

Strange noises were heard
By others who followed, bits of a tune
Coming in on loud weather

Though nothing like melody.
He blamed their fingers and ear
As unpractised, their fiddling easy

For he had gone alone into the island
And brought back the whole thing.
The house throbbed like his full violin.

So whether he calls it spirit music
Or not, I don't care. He took it
Out of wind off mid-Atlantic.

Still he maintains, from nowhere.
It comes off the bow gravely,
Rephrases itself into the air.

THOMAS HARDY

THE DARKLING THRUSH

—WRITTEN ON DECEMBER 31ST, 1900

I LEANT UPON A COPPICE GATE WHEN FROST WAS SPECTRE-GREY,

AND WINTER'S DREGS MADE DESOLATE THE WEAKENING EYE OF DAY.

THE TANGLED BINE-STEMS SCORED THE SKY
LIKE STRINGS OF BROKEN LYRES,

AND ALL MANKIND THAT HAUNTED NIGH
HAD SOUGHT THEIR HOUSEHOLD FIRES.

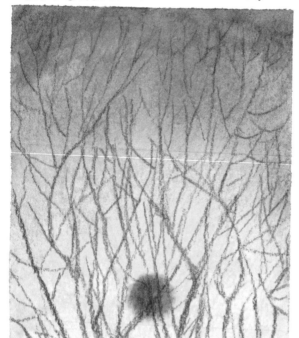 

THE LAND'S SHARP FEATURES SEEMED TO BE

THE CENTURY'S CORPSE OUTLEANT,

HIS CRYPT THE CLOUDY CANOPY, THE WIND HIS DEATH-LAMENT.

THE ANCIENT PULSE OF GERM AND BIRTH WAS SHRUNKEN HARD AND DRY,

AND EVERY SPIRIT UPON EARTH SEEMED FERVOURLESS AS I.

AT ONCE A VOICE AROSE AMONG
THE BLEAK TWIGS OVERHEAD

IN A FULL-HEARTED EVENSONG
OF JOY ILLIMITED;

AN AGED THRUSH, FRAIL, GAUNT, AND SMALL,
IN BLAST-BERUFFLED PLUME,

HAD CHOSEN THUS TO FLING HIS SOUL
                                UPON THE GROWING GLOOM.

SO LITTLE CAUSE FOR CAROLINGS
   OF SUCH ECSTATIC SOUND

WAS WRITTEN ON TERRESTRIAL THINGS
   AFAR OR NIGH AROUND,

THAT I COULD THINK THERE TREMBLED THROUGH
  HIS HAPPY GOOD-NIGHT AIR

SOME BLESSED HOPE, WHEREOF HE KNEW

AND I WAS UNAWARE.

THE DARKLING THRUSH

Thomas Hardy

I leant upon a coppice gate
    When Frost was spectre-grey,
And Winter's dregs made desolate
    The weakening eye of day.
The tangled bine-stems scored the sky
    Like strings of broken lyres,
And all mankind that haunted nigh
    Had sought their household fires.

The land's sharp features seemed to be
    The Century's corpse outleant,
His crypt the cloudy canopy,
    The wind his death-lament.
The ancient pulse of germ and birth
    Was shrunken hard and dry,
And every spirit upon earth
    Seemed fervourless as I.

At once a voice arose among
    The bleak twigs overhead
In a full-hearted evensong
    Of joy illimited;
An aged thrush, frail, gaunt, and small,
    In blast-beruffled plume,
Had chosen thus to fling his soul
    Upon the growing gloom.

So little cause for carolings
    Of such ecstatic sound
Was written on terrestrial things
    Afar or nigh around,
That I could think there trembled through
    His happy good-night air
Some blessed Hope, whereof he knew
    And I was unaware.

Seeing Nature

CHOICES

by TESS GALLAGHER

I GO TO THE MOUNTAIN SIDE

OF THE HOUSE TO CUT SAPLINGS,

AND CLEAR A VIEW TO SNOW

ON THE MOUNTAIN. BUT WHEN I LOOK UP,

SAW IN HAND, I SEE A NEST CLUTCHED IN THE UPPERMOST BRANCHES.

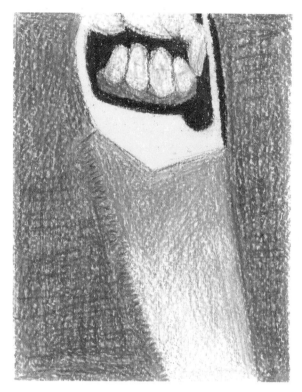

I DON'T CUT THAT ONE.

I DON'T CUT THE OTHERS EITHER.

SUDDENLY, IN EVERY TREE,

AN UNSEEN NEST

WHERE A MOUNTAIN WOULD BE.

CHOICES

Tess Gallagher

I go to the mountain side
of the house to cut saplings,
and clear a view to snow
on the mountain. But when I look up,
saw in hand, I see a nest clutched in
the uppermost branches.
I don't cut that one.
I don't cut the others either.
Suddenly, in every tree,
an unseen nest
where a mountain
would be.

THE FORCE THAT THROUGH THE GREEN FUSE DRIVES THE FLOWER

DRIVES MY GREEN AGE;

POEM BY DYLAN THOMAS

THAT BLASTS THE ROOTS OF TREES

IS MY DESTROYER.

AND I AM DUMB TO TELL THE CROOKED ROSE

MY YOUTH IS BENT BY THE SAME WINTRY FEVER.

THE LIPS OF TIME LEECH TO THE FOUNTAIN HEAD;
LOVE DRIPS AND GATHERS, BUT THE FALLEN BLOOD

SHALL CALM HER SORES.

AND I AM DUMB
TO TELL A WEATHER'S WIND

HOW TIME HAS TICKED A HEAVEN ROUND THE STARS.

AND I AM DUMB TO TELL THE LOVER'S TOMB

HOW AT MY SHEET GOES THE SAME CROOKED WORM.

THE FORCE THAT THROUGH THE GREEN FUSE DRIVES THE FLOWER

Dylan Thomas

The force that through the green fuse drives the flower
Drives my green age; that blasts the roots of trees
Is my destroyer.
And I am dumb to tell the crooked rose
My youth is bent by the same wintry fever.

The force that drives the water through the rocks
Drives my red blood; that dries the mouthing streams
Turns mine to wax.
And I am dumb to mouth unto my veins
How at the mountain spring the same mouth sucks.

The hand that whirls the water in the pool
Stirs the quicksand; that ropes the blowing wind
Hauls my shroud sail.
And I am dumb to tell the hanging man
How of my clay is made the hangman's lime.

The lips of time leech to the fountain head;
Love drips and gathers, but the fallen blood
Shall calm her sores.
And I am dumb to tell a weather's wind
How time has ticked a heaven round the stars.

And I am dumb to tell the lover's tomb
How at my sheet goes the same crooked worm.

Buffalo Dusk
by Carl Sandburg

drawings by
Julian Peters

THE BUFFALOES ARE GONE.

AND THOSE WHO SAW THE BUFFALOES ARE GONE.

THOSE WHO SAW THE BUFFALOES BY THOUSANDS AND HOW THEY PAWED THE PRAIRIE SOD

INTO DUST WITH THEIR HOOFS, THEIR GREAT HEADS DOWN PAWING ON IN A GREAT PAGEANT OF DUSK,

THOSE WHO SAW THE BUFFALOES ARE GONE.

AND THE BUFFALOES ARE GONE.

BUFFALO DUSK

Carl Sandburg

The buffaloes are gone.
And those who saw the buffaloes are gone.
Those who saw the buffaloes by thousands and how they pawed
    the prairie sod into dust with their hoofs, their great heads down
    pawing on in a great pageant of dusk,
Those who saw the buffaloes are gone.
And the buffaloes are gone.

THE WORLD IS TOO MUCH WITH US

by WILLIAM WORDSWORTH

the world is too much with us;

late and soon,

GETTING AND SPENDING,

we lay waste our powers;—

Little we see in Nature that is ours;

We have given our hearts away,

A Sordid Boon!

THIS SEA THAT BARES HER BOSOM TO THE MOON;
THE WINDS THAT WILL BE HOWLING AT ALL HOURS,

AND ARE UP-GATHERED NOW LIKE SLEEPING FLOWERS;

FOR THIS, FOR EVERYTHING, WE ARE OUT OF TUNE;

IT MOVES US NOT. GREAT GOD!
I'D RATHER BE
A PAGAN SUCKLED IN A CREED OUTWORN;

SO MIGHT I, STANDING ON THIS PLEASANT LEA,

HAVE GLIMPSES THAT WOULD MAKE ME LESS FORLORN;

HAVE SIGHT OF PROTEUS RISING FROM THE SEA;
OR HEAR OLD TRITON BLOW HIS WREATHÈD HORN.

The World Is Too Much with Us

William Wordsworth

The world is too much with us; late and soon,
Getting and spending, we lay waste our powers;—
Little we see in Nature that is ours;
We have given our hearts away, a sordid boon!
This Sea that bares her bosom to the moon;
The winds that will be howling at all hours,
And are up-gathered now like sleeping flowers;
For this, for everything, we are out of tune;
It moves us not. Great God! I'd rather be
A Pagan suckled in a creed outworn;
So might I, standing on this pleasant lea,
Have glimpses that would make me less forlorn;
Have sight of Proteus rising from the sea;
Or hear old Triton blow his wreathèd horn.

Seeing Time

HALF SUNK, A SHATTERED VISAGE LIES, WHOSE FROWN,

AND WRINKLED LIP, AND SNEER OF COLD COMMAND,

TELL THAT ITS SCULPTOR WELL THOSE PASSIONS READ

WHICH YET SURVIVE, STAMPED ON THESE LIFELESS THINGS,

THE HAND THAT MOCKED THEM, AND THE HEART THAT FED;

AND ON THE PEDESTAL, THESE WORDS APPEAR:

MY NAME IS OZYMANDIAS, KING OF KINGS;

LOOK ON MY WORKS, YE MIGHTY, AND DESPAIR!

NOTHING BESIDE REMAINS.
ROUND THE DECAY

OF THAT COLOSSAL WRECK,
BOUNDLESS AND BARE

THE LONE AND LEVEL SANDS STRETCH FAR AWAY."

OZYMANDIAS

Percy Bysshe Shelley

I met a traveller from an antique land,
Who said: "Two vast and trunkless legs of stone
Stand in the desert . . . Near them, on the sand,
Half sunk, a shattered visage lies, whose frown,
And wrinkled lip, and sneer of cold command,
Tell that its sculptor well those passions read
Which yet survive, stamped on these lifeless things,
The hand that mocked them, and the heart that fed:
And on the pedestal these words appear:
'My name is Ozymandias, king of kings:
Look on my works, ye mighty, and despair!'
Nothing beside remains. Round the decay
Of that colossal wreck, boundless and bare
The lone and level sands stretch far away."

THERE HAVE COME SOFT RAINS

A POEM BY JOHN PHILIP JOHNSON

IN KINDERGARTEN DURING THE COLD WAR,

MID-DAY LATE BELLS JOLTED US,

SENDING US SINGLE FILE INTO THE HALLWAY,

WHERE WE SAT, PRESSING OUR HEADS
BETWEEN OUR KNEES, WAITING.

DURING ONE OF THE BOMB DRILLS

ANNETTE WAS STANDING.

MY MOTHER SAID I WOULD TALK ON AND ON ABOUT HER, ABOUT HOW PRETTY SHE WAS.

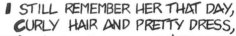

I STILL REMEMBER HER THAT DAY, CURLY HAIR AND PRETTY DRESS,

LOOKING PERTURBED THE WAY LITTLE CHILDREN DO.

WHY ANNETTE? THERE'S NOTHING TO BE UPSET ABOUT—

THE BOMBS WON'T GET US,

I'VE SEEN WHAT'S TO COME—

IT IS THE DAYS, THE STEADY

POUNDING OF DAYS, LIKE GENTLE RAIN,

THAT WILL BE OUR UNDOING.

There Have Come Soft Rains

John Philip Johnson

In kindergarten during the Cold War,
mid-day late bells jolted us,
sending us single file into the hallway,
where we sat, pressing our heads
between our knees, waiting.

During one of the bomb drills,
Annette was standing.
My mother said I would talk on and on
about her, about how pretty she was.
I still remember her that day,
curly hair and pretty dress,
looking perturbed the way
little children do.
Why Annette? There's nothing
to be upset about—
The bombs won't get us,
I've seen what's to come—
it is the days, the steady
pounding of days, like gentle rain,
that will be our undoing.

from BIRCHES by ROBERT FROST

SO WAS I ONCE MYSELF A
SWINGER OF BIRCHES.

AND SO I DREAM OF GOING
BACK TO BE.

IT'S WHEN I'M WEARY OF CONSIDERATIONS,
AND LIFE IS TOO MUCH LIKE A PATHLESS WOOD

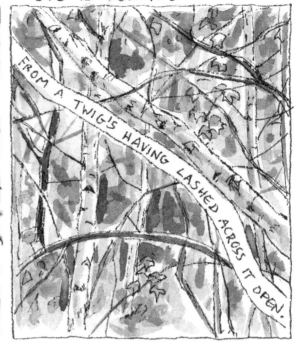

FROM A TWIG'S HAVING LASHED ACROSS IT OPEN.

I'D LIKE TO GET AWAY FROM
EARTH AWHILE

AND THEN COME BACK TO IT
AND BEGIN OVER.

MAY NO FATE WILLFULLY MISUNDERSTAND ME
AND HALF GRANT WHAT I WISH AND SNATCH ME AWAY

NOT TO RETURN. EARTH'S THE RIGHT PLACE FOR LOVE:
I DON'T KNOW WHERE IT'S LIKELY TO GO BETTER.

I'D LIKE TO GO BY CLIMBING A BIRCH TREE,

AND CLIMB BLACK BRANCHES UP A SNOW-WHITE TRUNK

TOWARD HEAVEN, TILL THE TREE COULD BEAR NO MORE,

BUT DIPPED ITS TOP

AND SET ME DOWN AGAIN.

THAT WOULD BE GOOD BOTH GOING AND COMING BACK.

ONE COULD DO WORSE THAN BE A SWINGER OF BIRCHES.

BIRCHES

Robert Frost

When I see birches bend to left and right
Across the lines of straighter darker trees,
I like to think some boy's been swinging them.
But swinging doesn't bend them down to stay
As ice-storms do. Often you must have seen them
Loaded with ice a sunny winter morning
After a rain. They click upon themselves
As the breeze rises, and turn many-colored
As the stir cracks and crazes their enamel.
Soon the sun's warmth makes them shed crystal shells
Shattering and avalanching on the snow-crust—
Such heaps of broken glass to sweep away
You'd think the inner dome of heaven had fallen.
They are dragged to the withered bracken by the load,
And they seem not to break; though once they are bowed
So low for long, they never right themselves:
You may see their trunks arching in the woods
Years afterwards, trailing their leaves on the ground
Like girls on hands and knees that throw their hair
Before them over their heads to dry in the sun.
But I was going to say when Truth broke in
With all her matter-of-fact about the ice-storm
I should prefer to have some boy bend them
As he went out and in to fetch the cows—
Some boy too far from town to learn baseball,
Whose only play was what he found himself,
Summer or winter, and could play alone.
One by one he subdued his father's trees
By riding them down over and over again
Until he took the stiffness out of them,
And not one but hung limp, not one was left

For him to conquer. He learned all there was
To learn about not launching out too soon
And so not carrying the tree away
Clear to the ground. He always kept his poise
To the top branches, climbing carefully
With the same pains you use to fill a cup
Up to the brim, and even above the brim.
Then he flung outward, feet first, with a swish,
Kicking his way down through the air to the ground.
So was I once myself a swinger of birches.
And so I dream of going back to be.
It's when I'm weary of considerations,
And life is too much like a pathless wood
Where your face burns and tickles with the cobwebs
Broken across it, and one eye is weeping
From a twig's having lashed across it open.
I'd like to get away from earth awhile
And then come back to it and begin over.
May no fate willfully misunderstand me
And half grant what I wish and snatch me away
Not to return. Earth's the right place for love:
I don't know where it's likely to go better.
I'd like to go by climbing a birch tree,
And climb black branches up a snow-white trunk
Toward heaven, till the tree could bear no more,
But dipped its top and set me down again.
That would be good both going and coming back.
One could do worse than be a swinger of birches.

Spring and Fall

by GERARD MANLEY HOPKINS

to a young child

MÁRGARÉT, ÁRE YOU GRÍEVING
OVER GOLDENGROVE UNLEAVING?

LEÁVES LIKE THE THINGS OF MAN, YOU

WITH YOUR FRESH THOUGHTS CARE FOR, CAN YOU?

AH! AS THE HEART GROWS OLDER
IT WILL COME TO SUCH
SIGHTS COLDER

BY AND BY, NOR SPARE A SIGH

THOUGH WORLDS OF WANWOOD LEAFMEAL LIE;

NOW NO MATTER, CHILD, THE NAME:

And yet
you will
weep and
know why.

SÓRROW'S SPRINGS ÁRE THE SAME.

NOR MOUTH HAD, NO NOR MIND, EXPRESSED WHAT HEART HEARD OF, GHOST GUESSED:

IT IS THE BLIGHT MAN WAS BORN FOR,

IT IS MARGARET YOU MOURN FOR.

Spring and Fall

Gerard Manley Hopkins

to a young child

Márgarét, áre you grieving
Over Goldengrove unleaving?
Leáves like the things of man, you
With your fresh thoughts care for, can you?
Ah! ás the heart grows older
It will come to such sights colder
By and by, nor spare a sigh
Though worlds of wanwood leafmeal lie;
And yet you wíll weep and know why.
Now no matter, child, the name:
Sórrow's spríngs áre the same.
Nor mouth had, no nor mind, expressed
What heart heard of, ghost guessed:
It ís the blight man was born for,
It is Margaret you mourn for.

Seeing Death

BEFORE THE BATTLE

by SIEGFRIED SASSOON

MUSIC OF WHISPERING TREES

HUSHED BY A BROAD-WINGED BREEZE

WHERE SHAKEN WATER GLEAMS;

AND EVENING RADIANCE FALLING

WITH REEDY BIRD-NOTES CALLING.

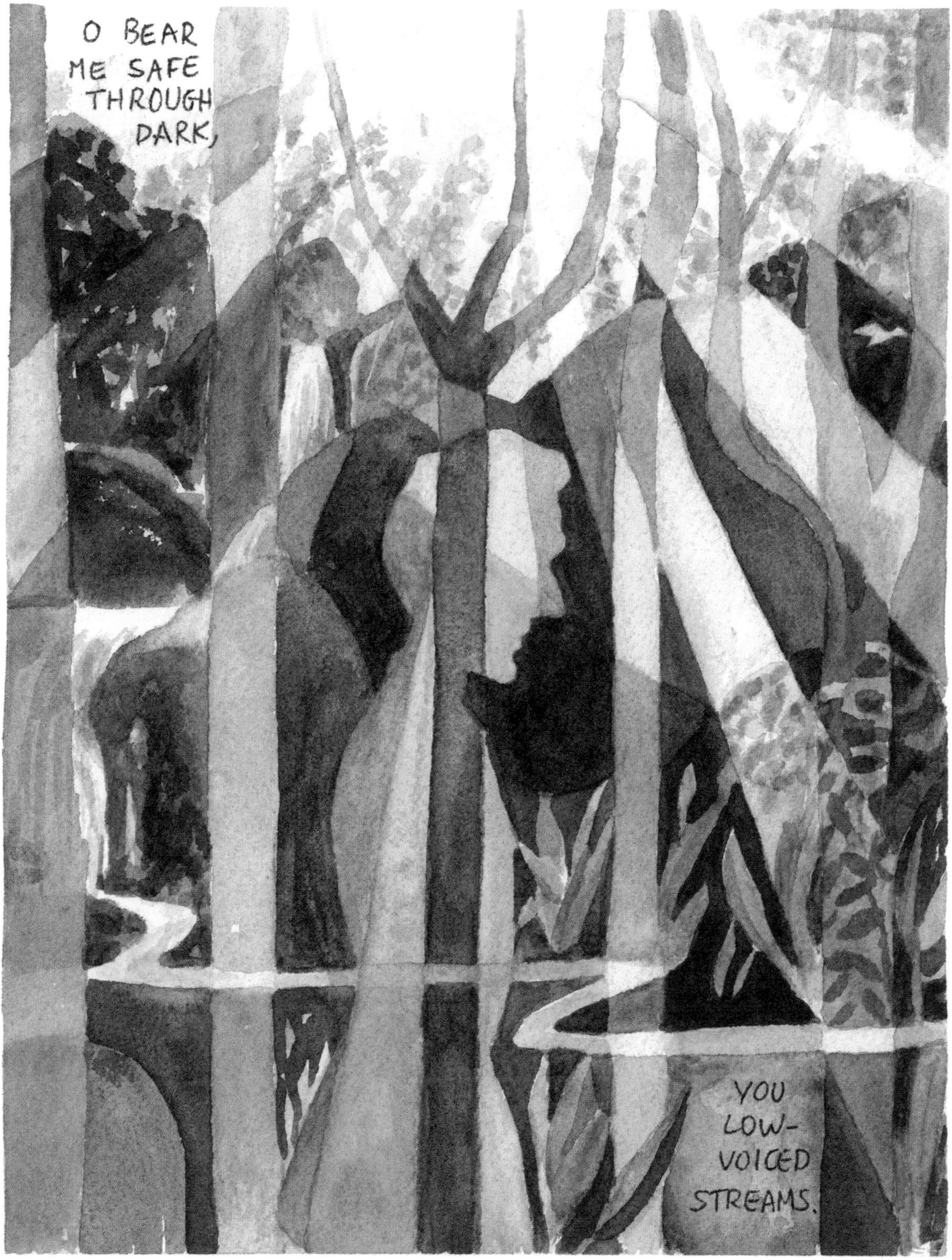
O BEAR
ME SAFE
THROUGH
DARK,
YOU
LOW-
VOICED
STREAMS.

I HAVE NO NEED TO PRAY

THAT FEAR MAY PASS AWAY;

I SCORN THE GROWL AND
RUMBLE OF THE FIGHT

THAT SUMMONS ME FROM COOL

SILENCE OF MARSH AND POOL

AND YELLOW LILIES
ISLANDED IN LIGHT

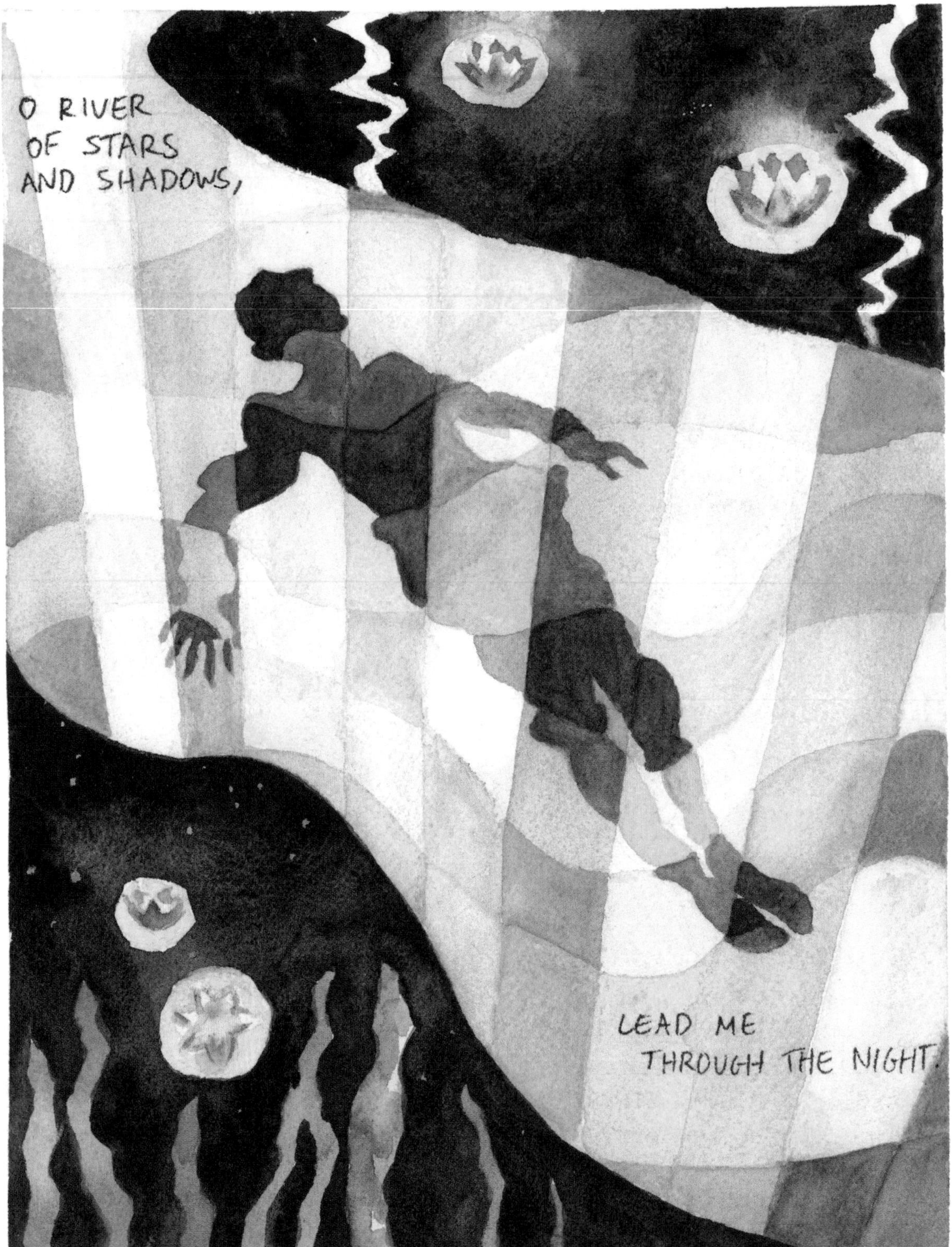
O RIVER
OF STARS
AND SHADOWS,
LEAD ME
THROUGH THE NIGHT.

Before the Battle

Siegfried Sassoon

Music of whispering trees
Hushed by a broad-winged breeze
Where shaken water gleams;
And evening radiance falling
With reedy bird-notes calling.
O Bear me safe through dark, you low-voiced streams.

I have no need to pray
That fear may pass away;
I scorn the growl and rumble of the fight
That summons me from cool
Silence of marsh and pool
And yellow lilies islanded in light
O river of stars and shadows, lead me through the night.

ANNABEL LEE

BY
EDGAR ALLAN
POE

IT WAS MANY AND MANY A YEAR AGO,

IN A KINGDOM BY THE SEA,

THAT A MAIDEN THERE LIVED WHOM YOU MAY KNOW

BY THE NAME OF ANNABEL LEE;

AND THIS MAIDEN SHE LIVED WITH NO OTHER THOUGHT THAN TO LOVE AND BE LOVED BY ME.

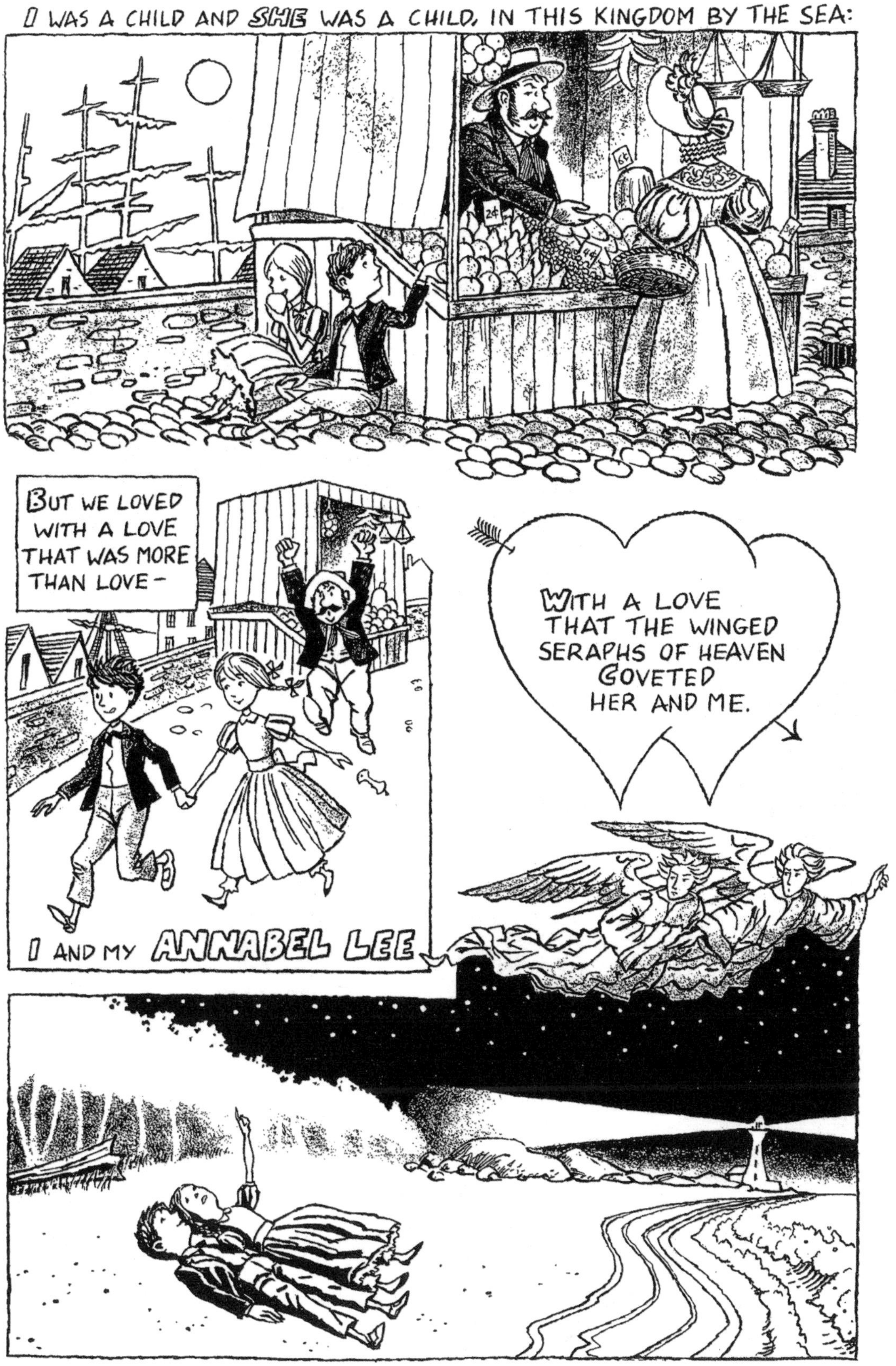
I WAS A CHILD AND SHE WAS A CHILD, IN THIS KINGDOM BY THE SEA:
BUT WE LOVED WITH A LOVE THAT WAS MORE THAN LOVE—
I AND MY ANNABEL LEE
WITH A LOVE THAT THE WINGED SERAPHS OF HEAVEN COVETED HER AND ME.

AND THIS WAS THE REASON THAT, LONG AGO, IN THIS KINGDOM BY THE SEA,

A WIND BLEW OUT OF A CLOUD,

CHILLING

MY BEAUTIFUL ANNABEL LEE;

SO THAT HER HIGH-BORN KINSMAN CAME AND BORE HER AWAY FROM ME,

TO SHUT HER UP IN A SEPULCHRE IN THIS KINGDOM BY THE SEA.

THE ANGELS, NOT HALF SO
HAPPY IN HEAVEN,
WENT ENVYING HER AND ME-

YES!-THAT WAS THE REASON

AS ALL MEN KNOW,
IN THIS KINGDOM
BY THE SEA

THAT THE WIND CAME OUT
OF THE CLOUD BY NIGHT,
CHILLING AND KILLING MY
ANNABEL LEE.

BUT OUR LOVE IT WAS STRONGER BY FAR THAN THE LOVE
◎F THOSE WHO WERE OLDER THAN WE—
◎F MANY FAR WISER THAN WE—

AND NEITHER
THE
ANGELS
IN HEAVEN
ABOVE,

NOR THE
DEMONS DOWN UNDER
THE SEA,

CAN EVER DISSEVER
MY SOUL FROM THE SOUL

OF THE BEAUTIFUL
ANNABEL LEE,

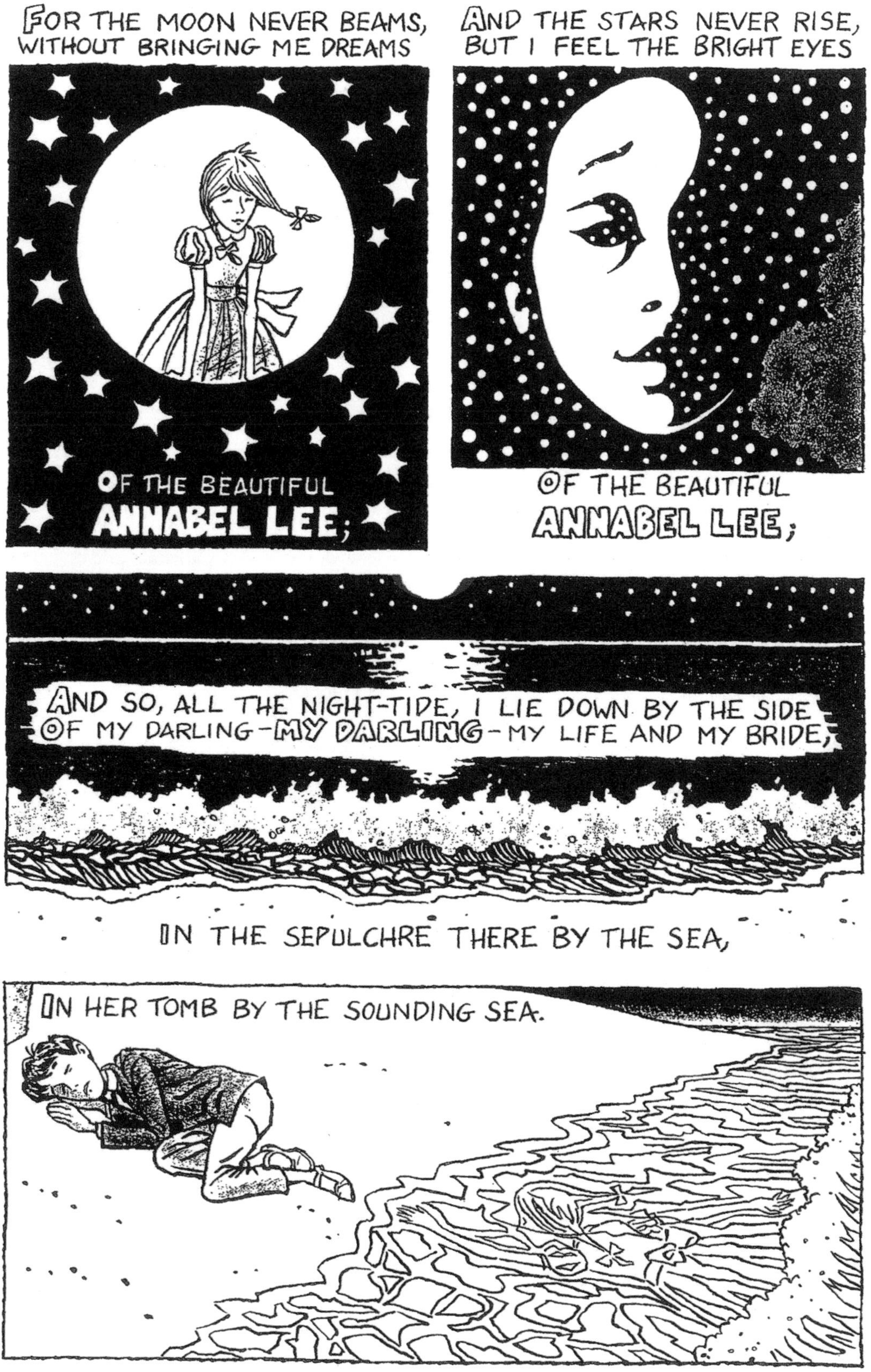
FOR THE MOON NEVER BEAMS, WITHOUT BRINGING ME DREAMS
OF THE BEAUTIFUL ANNABEL LEE;
AND THE STARS NEVER RISE, BUT I FEEL THE BRIGHT EYES
OF THE BEAUTIFUL ANNABEL LEE;
AND SO, ALL THE NIGHT-TIDE, I LIE DOWN BY THE SIDE OF MY DARLING—MY DARLING—MY LIFE AND MY BRIDE,
IN THE SEPULCHRE THERE BY THE SEA,
IN HER TOMB BY THE SOUNDING SEA.

ANNABEL LEE

Edgar Allan Poe

It was many and many a year ago,
   In a kingdom by the sea,
That a maiden there lived whom you may know
   By the name of Annabel Lee;
And this maiden she lived with no other thought
   Than to love and be loved by me.

I was a child and she was a child,
   In this kingdom by the sea,
But we loved with a love that was more than love—
   I and my Annabel Lee—
With a love that the wingèd seraphs of Heaven
   Coveted her and me.

And this was the reason that, long ago,
   In this kingdom by the sea,
A wind blew out of a cloud, chilling
   My beautiful Annabel Lee;
So that her highborn kinsmen came
   And bore her away from me,
To shut her up in a sepulcher
   In this kingdom by the sea.

The angels, not half so happy in Heaven,
   Went envying her and me—
Yes!—that was the reason (as all men know,
   In this kingdom by the sea)
That the wind came out of the cloud by night,
   Chilling and killing my Annabel Lee.

But our love it was stronger by far than the love
    Of those who were older than we—
    Of many far wiser than we—
And neither the angels in Heaven above
    Nor the demons down under the sea
Can ever dissever my soul from the soul
    Of the beautiful Annabel Lee;

For the moon never beams, without bringing me dreams
    Of the beautiful Annabel Lee;
And the stars never rise, but I feel the bright eyes
    Of the beautiful Annabel Lee;
And so, all the night-tide, I lie down by the side
    Of my darling—my darling—my life and my bride,
    In her sepulchre there by the sea—
    In her tomb by the sounding sea.

BECAUSE I COULD NOT STOP FOR
DEATH —

HE KINDLY STOPPED FOR ME—

THE CARRIAGE HELD BUT JUST
OURSELVES —

AND IMMORTALITY.

WE SLOWLY DROVE – HE KNEW NO HASTE

AND I HAD PUT AWAY
MY LABOR AND MY LEISURE TOO,

FOR HIS CIVILITY—

WE PASSED THE SCHOOL, WHERE CHILDREN STROVE
AT RECESS – IN THE RING—

WE PASSED THE FIELDS OF
GAZING GRAIN—

WE PASSED THE SETTING SUN—

OR RATHER—HE PASSED US—

THE DEWS DREW QUIVERING
AND CHILL—

FOR ONLY GOSSAMER, MY GOWN—

MY TIPPET—ONLY TULLE—

WE PAUSED BEFORE A HOUSE THAT SEEMED
A SWELLING OF THE GROUND—

THE ROOF WAS SCARCELY VISIBLE—

THE CORNICE—IN THE GROUND—

SINCE THEN — 'TIS CENTURIES —
AND YET

FEELS SHORTER THAN THE DAY

I FIRST SURMISED THE HORSES' HEADS
WERE TOWARD ETERNITY —

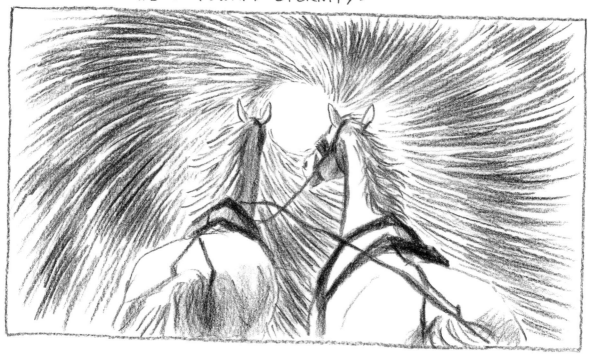

BECAUSE I COULD NOT STOP FOR DEATH

Emily Dickinson

Because I could not stop for Death –
He kindly stopped for me –
The Carriage held but just Ourselves –
And Immortality.

We slowly drove – He knew no haste
And I had put away
My labor and my leisure too,
For His Civility –

We passed the School, where Children strove
At Recess – in the Ring –
We passed the Fields of Gazing Grain –
We passed the Setting Sun –

Or rather – He passed us –
The Dews drew quivering and chill –
For only Gossamer, my Gown –
My Tippet – only Tulle –

We paused before a House that seemed
A Swelling of the Ground –
The Roof was scarcely visible –
The Cornice – in the Ground –

Since then – 'tis Centuries – and yet
Feels shorter than the Day
I first surmised the Horses' Heads
Were toward Eternity –

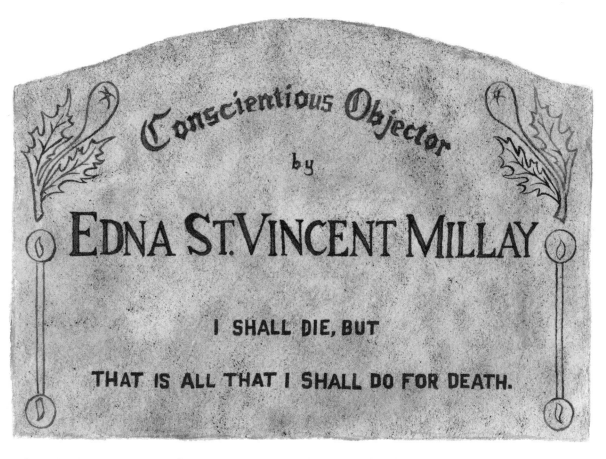

Conscientious Objector

by

EDNA ST.VINCENT MILLAY

I SHALL DIE, BUT

THAT IS ALL THAT I SHALL DO FOR DEATH.

I HEAR HIM LEADING HIS HORSE OUT OF THE STALL;

I HEAR THE CLATTER ON THE BARN-FLOOR.

HE IS IN HASTE; HE HAS
BUSINESS IN CUBA,

BUSINESS IN THE BALKANS, MANY
CALLS TO MAKE THIS MORNING.

BUT I WILL NOT HOLD THE BRIDLE

WHILE HE CLINCHES THE GIRTH.

AND HE MAY MOUNT BY HIMSELF:

I WILL NOT GIVE HIM A LEG UP.

THOUGH HE FLICK MY SHOULDERS WITH HIS WHIP,

I WILL NOT TELL HIM WHICH WAY THE FOX RAN.

WITH HIS HOOF ON MY BREAST, I WILL NOT TELL HIM WHERE THE BLACK BOY HIDES IN THE SWAMP.

I SHALL DIE, BUT THAT IS ALL THAT I SHALL DO FOR DEATH;

I AM NOT ON HIS PAY-ROLL.

I WILL NOT TELL HIM THE WHEREABOUTS OF MY FRIENDS

NOR OF MY ENEMIES EITHER.

THOUGH HE PROMISE ME MUCH,

I WILL NOT MAP HIM THE ROUTE TO ANY MAN'S DOOR.

AM I A SPY IN THE LAND OF THE LIVING,

THAT I SHOULD DELIVER MEN TO DEATH?

BROTHER, THE PASSWORD AND THE PLANS OF OUR CITY

ARE SAFE WITH ME; NEVER THROUGH ME SHALL YOU BE OVERCOME.

Conscientious Objector

Edna St. Vincent Millay

I shall die, but
that is all that I shall do for Death.
I hear him leading his horse out of the stall;
I hear the clatter on the barn-floor.
He is in haste; he has business in Cuba,
business in the Balkans, many calls to make this morning.
But I will not hold the bridle
while he clinches the girth.
And he may mount by himself:
I will not give him a leg up.

Though he flick my shoulders with his whip,
I will not tell him which way the fox ran.
With his hoof on my breast, I will not tell him where
the black boy hides in the swamp.
I shall die, but that is all that I shall do for Death;
I am not on his pay-roll.

I will not tell him the whereabout of my friends
nor of my enemies either.
Though he promise me much,
I will not map him the route to any man's door.
Am I a spy in the land of the living,
that I should deliver men to Death?
Brother, the password and the plans of our city
are safe with me; never through me
Shall you be overcome.

Sources

Emily Dickinson, "'Hope' Is the Thing with Feathers," from *Poems: Second Series* (Boston: Robert Brothers, 1891).

William Ernest Henley, "Invictus," from *A Book of Verses* (London: David Nutt, 1888).

Maya Angelou, "Caged Bird," from *Shaker, Why Don't You Sing?* (New York: Random House, 1983). Copyright © 1983 by Maya Angelou. Used by permission of Random House, an imprint and division of Penguin Random House LLC, and by permission of Virago Press, an imprint of Little, Brown Book Group, Ltd. All rights reserved.

e. e. cummings, "may my heart always be open," from *Complete Poems: 1904–1962*, edited by George J. Firmage (New York: Liveright, 1991). Copyright © 1938, 1966, 1991 by the Trustees for the E. E. Cummings Trust. Used by permission of Liveright Publishing Corporation.

Christina Rossetti, "Somewhere or Other," from *The Prince's Progress and Other Poems* (London: Macmillan, 1866).

Robert Hayden, "Those Winter Sundays," from *Collected Poems of Robert Hayden*, edited by Frederick Glaysher (New York: Liveright, 1985). Copyright © 1966 by Robert Hayden. Used by permission of Liveright Publishing Corporation.

Ezra Pound, "In a Station of the Metro," from *Poetry* (April 1913).

W. B. Yeats, "When You Are Old," from *The Rose* (1893). Digital screentone effects by Maryse Daniel.

Langston Hughes, "Juke Box Love Song" from *The Collected Poems of Langston Hughes*, edited by Arnold Rampersad with David Roessel, associate editor (New York: Knopf, 1994). Copyright © 1994 by the Estate of Langston Hughes. Used by permission of Alfred A. Knopf, an imprint of the Knopf Doubleday Publishing Group, a division of Penguin Random House LLC, and by permission of Harold Ober Associates. All rights reserved.

W. H. Auden, "Musée des Beaux Arts," from *Another Time* (New York: Random House, 1940). Copyright © 1940 and copyright renewed 1968 by W. H. Auden. Used by permission of Random House, an imprint and division of Penguin Random House LLC, and by permission of Curtis Brown, Ltd. All rights reserved.

Seamus Heaney, "The Given Note," from *Door into the Dark* (London: Faber and Faber, 1972). Reprinted by permission of Faber and Faber, Ltd.

Thomas Hardy, "The Darkling Thrush," from *Poems of the Past and the Present* (London and New York: Harper, 1902).

Tess Gallagher, "Choices," from *Midnight Lantern: New and Selected Poems* (Minneapolis: Graywolf Press, 2011). Copyright © 2006 by Tess Gallagher. Reprinted with the permission of The Permissions Company, LLC on behalf of the author and Graywolf Press, Minneapolis, Minnesota, www.graywolf-press.org.

Dylan Thomas, "The Force That through the Green Fuse Drives the Flower," from *The Poems of Dylan Thomas* (New York: New Directions, 1953). Copyright © 1939 by New Directions Publishing Corp. Reprinted by permission of New Directions Publishing Corp. Copyright © 1937 by The Dylan Thomas Trust. Reprinted outside the United States by permission of David Higham Associates.

Carl Sandburg, "Buffalo Dusk," from *Smoke and Steel* (New York: Harcourt, Brace and Co, 1921).

William Wordsworth, "The World Is Too Much with Us," from *Poems, in Two Volumes* (London: Longman, Hurst, Rees, and Orme, 1807).

Percy Bysshe Shelley, "Ozymandias," from *Rosalind and Helen, A Modern Eclogue; With Other Poems* (London: C. and J. Ollier, 1819).

John Philip Johnson, "There Have Come Soft Rains," from *Rattle* No. 45 (Fall 2014). Poem copyright © 2014 by John Philip Johnson. Reprinted by permission of John Philip Johnson.

Robert Frost, "Birches," from *Mountain Interval* (New York: Henry Holt, 1916).

Gerard Manley Hopkins, "Spring and Fall," written 1880, first published in *Poems of Gerard Manley Hopkins* (London: H. Milford, 1918).

Siegfried Sassoon, "Before the Battle," from *The War Poems of Siegfried Sassoon* (London: W. Heinemann, 1919).

Edgar Allan Poe, "Annabel Lee," first published in the *New York Daily Tribune*, October 9, 1849, two days after Poe's death.

Emily Dickinson, "Because I Could Not Stop for Death," from *Poems of Emily Dickinson* (Boston: Robert Brothers, 1890).

Edna St. Vincent Millay, "Conscientious Objector," from *Wine from these Grapes* (New York: Harper and Bros, 1934). Copyright © 1934, 1962 by Edna St. Vincent Millay and Norma Millay Ellis. Reprinted with the permission of The Permissions Company, LLC on behalf of Holly Peppe, Literary Executor, The Edna St. Vincent Millay Society. www.millay.org.

Julian Peters' illustrations of "Those Winter Sundays," "The Given Note," "Buffalo Dusk," and "Before the Battle" first appeared in *Plough Quarterly*. www.plough.com